EVER

a novella by

BLAKE BUTLER

ISBN-13: 978-0-9798080-6-7
ISBN-10: 0-9798080-6-5

Thanks to the editors of *Unsaid* and *Tarpaulin Sky*,
where excerpts of EVER previously appeared.

Thanks to DW, PM, GL, BATB, LDB, MK, HND,
BE and MM.

Cover and accompanying art/designs by Derek White.

Published by Calamari Press, Nairobi/Detroit

www.calamaripress.com

For my mother and her mother

For my father

[From in the light I touched the light. I knew the light grew mold inside me.

   [Or.

      [Or what. I could not think.]]

I could not find]   ]   ]]]]

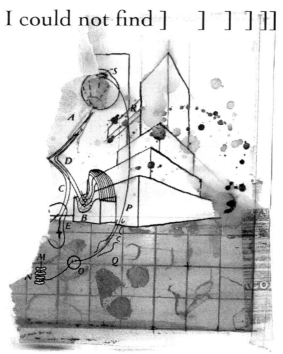

[I could not find the wall. In the long small straight of where I'd been I could look back and see some lurking, yet in the light I'd pause for hours and hear no other inhale, no clicky-clack. In the light my skin was see-through—my veins an atlas spanned in tissue. I'd never been much for direction. The wind would wind my hair. I once got lost in my own district and had to beat my head on unmarked doors. Most of the homes remained undaunted, silent, though one man answered in his flesh—bright white and ripped with rashing. I tried to understand.

[I tried to move among the light forgiven. I kept low, crouched in case of flux—i.e.: slips or divots in the foundation, or even, on my own part: dizzy, dumb. I walked and walked and walked and light continued farther on.]

[When I could not walk, I settled briefly, bargained. I let my head against the tile. In certain spots I heard a humming, some long slow strum sung through the floor. At times it mimicked Mother's tumor babble: nights I'd wake inside the house inside her howl, or humping hard against a bare wall, leaving wet imprints on the plaster. The way her eyes went curtained, glassy, as she spoke by scratching in my hand. In that light, there—where?—I felt her underneath me, goner, growing, on.

 [For certain lengths I crawled, no rube to the position.]

 [For certain lengths I simply suggested myself forward. I felt the tremor of small bees. I kissed the ground in want of _____. When I could not crawl or want or other, I crooked my arms and hid my head in what remained of me.]]

[Behind my eyes the light went on.]]]

[Meanwhile, in the outside, during certain weeks the air would fold. The light comprising certain sections of certain rooms would burst or bubble. Strings of night might gleam of glass. The dirt would swim with foam. Sometimes there'd be forewarning—a small eruption, more luminescence, an ache or hum of heat in rising steam—though you couldn't recognize the warping till you'd lost a hand or head. I mean the sky could lift your skin off. The air would shift like some fucked puzzle. Whole bird flocks might be witnessed flying, say, into the ridge over the field of refuse stacked sky-high behind my house, and then those birds would disappear or become fire or melt away to sludge.

  [I'd been in the front yard digging for what I'd lost once when I saw a yawning eat a bus of healthy children.

    [I'd seen on TV as the fifty-yard line became a blister and all those padded men smeared to zero—how quick the broadcast went to blackness and then the blackness went to fuzz and then the fuzz went to an ad for breakfast sausage, which I must say looked quite delicious.]

    [I saw across the sun a slightly trembling meniscus just above us, above our home and smothered city, where like my mother I grew into a woman in this home.]]

[At first our local leaders tried to zone around the madness, to block off damaged sects with panes of glass, but the error swung so often, the glass just magnified the problem—the shatter echoed in the ground.

[There were other kinds of trouble. Somewhere the rifts let others in. Bodies burped from out of nowhere. Men with names no one had heard. They looked like most other people, except kind. They knew of nowhere else to go. They'd climb trees until the limbs snapped, or lay on hot concrete in hope of numb, or spin continuously in circles, or work their whole arms down their throats. The air gone. The gutter lard another color. At night the streets were clogged. Soon you couldn't buy bread or gum or condoms, no matter how much you wanted, how much you'd pay.]]

[And in my home too, every morning, there were people. Crammed in the air around my bed, or locked above it, embezzled in my bedclothes or in the closet crack, in the lightbulb's frying wires, in my hair, my awful teeth.

   [These days I sleep with steak knives, grow my nails out. I'm saving money for a gun.]]

[On the news they showed the woman who'd lost her baby to the yawning in her sock drawer. They showed the high school cafeteria where the whole hot lunch line became sucked under, bystanders splotched with taco glop. They showed the river where another fold had slurred the water, where fish were turning into blood.

   [They did not show the miles of freeway caressed in plastic, meant to contain the spread of things we'd breathed.

9

[They did not show the way the trees had took to growing sideways, looking for the light, or hung with fat so black and bulged the limbs bent, weak.]

[They did not show my face, so scratched I shouldn't mention.]

[They did not show the beach agleam with crawl.]]

[I'd heard there were centers somewhere where the ruined got rubbed with creams on tables, fed forever. I heard another about a canopy they were building, somewhere somewhat, a reflective roof over us all.

[Some said inside the 3rd stall on the right in a men's room off a certain exit of I-285 the light could make you young.]]

[I heard these things and wrote them down.

[I spread these rumors through the house—in my hemlines, on my forehead, along the margins of my books, across the bedroom ceiling that I might look up and in certain moments imagine something somewhere; that I might hope or muse or glean, might even grin a little, might remember, though my handwriting is shit.]]]]

[My mother's house had gone on standing despite the nights of cracking sky. I'd hear the roof split open in my sleep but in the morning we were there. The neighbors, meanwhile, suffered. The wet and muck and sleet and slats of blackened crud left several shacks or mansions half-dismantled. Office buildings downtown became sucked under. Grids were slipped to sliding. The list of lost went on: parking decks and patios and poolhalls and party buses and daycares full of babies made of fat. Food courts and tree houses and sanitation yards and outlet malls. Strip bars and coffee shops and trampolines and used car lots. Whole islands. Chinese diners. Laundromats and high schools and pickle vendors and manufacturers of baubles. Skylong fields of corn. Oceans. Winter. It all went under. It made bubbles. Some bubbles were given names. I'm not sure where the rest all ended up, or what about it. I'm not sure what it was about my dad or me or mother that had kept us whole, unbuttered, slightly longer, though Mother swore among her final claps of cleaner English how our home had been protected. That through her green knees and praising pages, the shrines she'd installed in every bedroom, the blood breakfast, the grief she'd spilled into my father, the black nettle switch my legs had took the brunt of, the half Dad's paychecks she mailed to nowhere — that all of this had made us rich. Not rich in candled dinners, though, or sleeping quarters or things driven into town, not rich in the things average people wanted — rich in *our becoming*, my mother said. She could barely form the words. My mother's mouth a little raw or crowded. *Rich in the coming day's new skin.* Her teeth clenched as she stammered. She'd try to bite me. And oh, the glisten in her cheek skin, watching the Mathers and the Murmans and the Meads and who all ever else in no squat radii go under and/or crumple and/or die. Mom, who wore that glimmer on to heaven or wherever. Who wore her eyes open going under, even, once that mud, briefly delayed, covered her over, negating the previous suspicion.

[In mother's absence, our front yard never henceforth grew. Though in the bugs that came to grovel, grieving, smothered, well... well nothing. God. Goodnight.]]

[No, nevermind. I will continue with the telling if you swear forgiveness in the end. Not that you want, or even matter, or me, or them, or which, or—stop.]

[There are thirteen plastic doors in this house, and I have been through none. None have hinges, handles, or keyholes. Only some have knobs.

[Sometimes when I am careful I hear people talk through certain of the doors.]]

[The door in the kitchen pantry is the first one I found. I was after something to feed the neighbor's cat, whom I hadn't seen in weeks, but I could plan. The door was four feet high and the color of the wall. I cleared the cans and boxes and removed the shelving. I put my face against the door's. It would not open. I knocked and knocked. I got on hands and knees to peer beneath. I could not see anything but light.

[Other people lived inside this house before me. I do not regret my time alone.]

[I often like to eat my dinner in the mirror and pretend I'm watching someone else.]]

[The door inside the coat closet shudders and sometimes there is scratching.

  [The door inside the cabinet under the guest bedroom sink has a pattern on its face.]]

[I frequently receive calls from a woman who asks and asks to speak to the man of the house.

  [For weeks all my outgoing mail came back *return to sender*.]

  [I like to take pictures and hide the film.]]

[The door under my bed is installed with a small window. Through the window I can see into another family's home. I watch them eat breakfast and clean the dishes and discuss the matters of the house. They do not know I can see them. Or if they do, they don't let on.

[Once someone knocked on the door inside the dishwasher. It shook the counter and threw a picture off the wall. The dishwasher was on heated dry cycle and I did not want to open it in fear I'd burn my hand. By the time the cycle ended, there was no knock.

  [The door in the floor in the sunroom changes colors with the weather.

    [I have heard there are men and women who fantasize of rape.]

    [I try not to believe everything I am told but there is often too much time to think.]]

[When I receive a call from a wrong number I try to keep them on the line as long as possible.]]

[I took a screwdriver to the door in my attic. I broke three fingernails and scratched the paint. I went to the hardware store and bought a pickaxe. I chipped and chapped and swung. I could feel the burn in my arms for weeks. I hid the pickaxe in the closet.

[I once received a photo of myself in the mail with no return address. I had no idea who took it or where or when. I was smiling in the picture. I looked well, in admiration. I stuck the photo on the fridge with magnets with my eyes facing the front door.]]

[One of the doors is a pet entrance I had installed though I do not own a dog or cat. I would get one but I once heard about a friend who was mauled to death by his cocker spaniel.]

[I like to keep my options open.]

[Sometimes at night I hear certain doors open and people come into my house. I am usually already in bed or in the bathtub when this happens. Nothing is ever missing or misplaced.

[I take that back: one night my silk gloves had been put on by someone with large hands. The silk was all stretched out and I could no longer wear them. I still keep them in a drawer.]]

[I was informed at a young age I would not have children.]

[I don't like to wear the same outfit more than once a year.]]

[The only door I ever went through was in the crawlspace under the den. It was unlocked and came right open. Behind the door, there was the light. There was a corridor. The air was cool. There weren't any other doors or pictures. It went on and on and on.

[The door beside my front door confuses me when I am tired.]

[There are several large bumps beneath my hair.]]

[I dreamt there was a door inside my stomach. It was gray and had a curtained window. I could feel the doorbell on my tongue.

[Some nights in bed I'll lay with my face pressed against the door lodged in my headboard and I will hold my breath and I will listen.

[Other nights I sleep.]]]

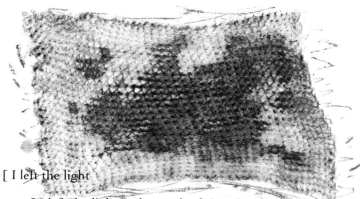

[I left the light

[I left the light and came back into it. Into here, to us.

[Came back in the house, back-cracked and brain brayed. The walls whitewashed and very near.]

[I'd bled a thread across my shirt unknowing, the cotton soaked clean through—clumping caked all in my tangles—a gross condition earned from younger years, when often I could not keep my head from shaking no. Most evenings still I'll bleed at least a tiny rind or crusting mostly from my ears, though sometimes there comes a curtain and sometimes with brute force.

[When I slept with cotton in my ear holes (which also helped conceal the roof's in-caving creak, the gunfire and the shouting), the blood would gush up from my nostrils or an older bruise, even those considered healed. Or from my vagina (even in off-times). Or my knuckles or my mouth. Some days I'd wake to find the pillow sopping, chock full and black around the edges.

23

[The blood would always find a way.]]]]

[From the window came new light. I went and pressed myself against it. Children were rolling in the liquid. Another crack had caused a local lake to reroute through our yard. Bits of crud and skin and other hung on the foaming surface, like a bib. In certain places on the water you could stand. *You might also walk forever in one particular direction, if you knew each inching way to creep.* The kids had thrown themselves among the muck along the river's lip where the grass had turned into hive paper. There were seven children left now, one less than last week. Another brother had fallen off the roof trying to reach the gleaming that'd opened up above their house. Inside, his insides were all mush.

[These kids remaining weren't distracted. They let the sores run in their eyes. They had a dog they'd caught from somewhere. They held it together off the ground. There were divots in the dog's ribcage, the weird flesh where cysts had entered, a mangy rind of matted patterns in his coat. Beneath the skin something was wadded. The dog's ass also gave off blood. Around the boys the black straps the city had used to keep the remaining trees alive and upright vibrated in hot wind. The sun flicked on and off and on. The kids looked up to me briefly, their pupils spinning, nostrils clogged and skin shellacked. They could see. I closed the curtain. I turned around and touched my lids. I said a prayer—a wish whispered less for them or me or the dog or yard, and more for everything at once.

[When that prayer was over I began again.]]]

24

[When that prayer was over I began again.

  [When that prayer was over I began again.

   [When that prayer was over I began again.]

[I hadn't meant to speak in repetition; and yet did so out of something in me wanting. By the fifth instance the words slurred slightly, skewed from my original intention — and yet I did not pause or cause correction. I spoke into the room and felt it fill. My voice sounded only slightly off. Some scrunched foundation in me, gonging. The itch ripped in my throat. My spit came up in long black strands. Susurration in my vision. I touched my throat bulb. The thing was thrumming. I spoke an awful language. I heard myself confess to things I had not done.

  [I told myself to find the door.]

[I moved towards the door that held the outside, where I could taste the air the way it was—*wart and charcoal and skin powder*—but as I neared the door—*not me moving but something moving me*—I began to feel heavy and more tired, more dumb and dumb and dumb—*inflating*—until at one point, short of exit, I found myself curled in the floor, cramped and breathing harder than I'd ever, so hard I couldn't see—*not that I'd want to or that it mattered*—so hard I felt my teeth would jar out and open, skunked with guggle.]]]

[I could see the door still a little.

  [I could—still could—see the door.

  [Door(s)(s).

    [Def.: *door* (n): 1. a thing I'd noticed.

      [2. A thing through once I'd—

        [once I'd—been.]]]]]]

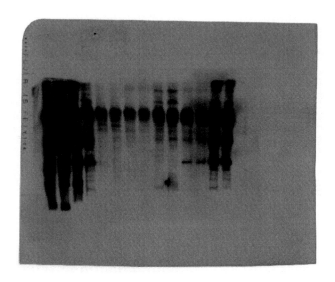

[In the floor I lay for hours watching the wall that it might open. I pressed my face against the paint to listen. I blew my breath to keep me warm. If I could blow enough to cause a puncture I would try to fit into the gap. The room was cold, no matter how much I had the clothes on, and more clothes. I could feel the excess in the bits I'd covered best, where the skin fit to the ridge. I'd put my father's deathbed jacket on. A stain on the right arm sleeve of something lighter colored, not quite yellow not quite white. The foamy pump of the coat's wristlets touched high up on my hand.

[What had my father done inside this jacket.]

[What had my mother seen him do.

[What nights would yawn around them, laced, somewhere before me, clogged in years.]]]

[I was so thick now I could hardly feel me, except in the places said above. In the weird light through the window I could crane my head at an angle with the floor. I'd set my forehead crooked to the texture at its softest point, my teeth girders for my skull. In this configuration I could see the way the wall wished to leave itself, the house. I could see the swell of it, the waver. Even parts in glisten where my fingers, oiled unconscious, had touched and left my remnant now, some small betrayal.

[I pushed my head harder on the carpet. Pushed my head harder. Pushed.]]

[Someone was knocking on the door.]

[Someone was knocking. I curled. I counted. I pressed my knee against my knee. I scrunched as small as I could manage. No one had come in since the wind. I felt a pressure. Some unscrewing. In the rhythm between knocking I squirmed a little further till I was flat against the floor. My skin stuck to the wall as I came off it. I felt the painted plaster leave a rind.

[Someone was there. Someone with fingers. *Had he or she seen me in the light?*

[He.]

[He.]

[He.]]]

[In the silence slurring through here, I settled each shortened section of me further for the house. I felt so fat from all my layers I did not have to worry with disease — the hair, the bugs, the skin cells, the rotting other.

  [Up close the carpet stunk. I held my breath to keep it off me.]

  [I asked to have this knocking taken from my door. To know no whole. I pressed my teeth against my teeth. The keyhole saw me writhing.]

  [I'd thought I'd wanted this before. I'd asked and asked for years and hours somewhere someone. Now in the blip my body suffered. My muscles made a moor. The knocking beat against my cheeks. I could not keep me firm.

    [*The house never not knowing.*]]]

[There were new windows in the house. Fixed along the low end of the curled wall where the water'd warped. Through the windows I saw swollen birds implode. I saw deer molding in tremendous rain, the gulping yard, the grog, and among this, in the gone grass, a massive tree I'd once dreamt of sawing over, it went bent so far its branches splintered, splattered, popcorned into pus. I saw several sections of the ground go puckered — portals in. I did not see anyone return.

  [My eye began to crimp — the meat intoning —

    [my own fold opening in me —]]]

The door, when stubbed, made my teeth ache.

[No matter how or when or which way, the knock would not appear again. Though I'd known something of my neighbor in his vision, and was sure it'd been him who left that thing outside my door—the thing I'd rather not now give a name—and though I swore to myself aloud at length for weeks in waiting that when he reappeared this time I'd come—he did not appear. He did not move through me in the ways I'd only shortly saw I wanted. Some nights I would flicker. Some nights I'd taste him in the frozen food that I'd defrosted. Hear him speaking in low monotonic when I ran the bathwater—silent after. I felt him behind me, often sweating, the bug of his breath a metronome, though never, near not, never.

[Days I'd stand outside his home. In the runned slush our common yards had made, I'd sometimes straddle the soft spots with both feet. I'd wait and breathe and squeeze my fingers. If I took my shoes out of my slippers and touched the mud, I'd imagine ways to sink into it — such depths for doors — an enveloping. The makeshift moon — a state-made blinker — above would crud its colors, the sorts of shades you would not want above. The glass of the house glistened flat, and with my head at certain angles, I could sometimes see faces in the glare. This man was even on the far side of parts not left translucent — the walls, the eaves, the air. Smoke often gushed up from the soil bed, another form of leaving. The stink of scorching laced into it. The insects' spurt from some earth's sneeze. I stretched each moment to its thinnest, knowing when I'd turn, there he would be.

   [You should know — I did not go on without clear signals. The man was in my teeth. I heard him among those rung above me when I lay sleeping, wrapped in sheets. And the thing he'd left me sitting on my front porch a bauble, really — a node or nodule, or an eye — this thing would grow warm with my squeezing. It would fizzle on my palm. If I held it long enough and in the right way it would cause sores to well up under my skin. Huge bright and bulging wafers, soft as water. Rashes rouged across my neck. Sometimes I woke up with catlike scratching on my lips or knees or up my back. Though at first I'd slept with the thing nuzzled to my stomach, I now left it sitting on the dresser. I could feel it from there watching, its blinkless want boring my sides. Even when I had to turn it to face the far wall, I could not bring myself to make it leave me, or give it over, be destroyed.]

31

[This thing, it had me in it, and I could not make us unpeel.]]

[Other times, I would slink into the other house. It required only a certain configuration of controlled movement. I timed the distance with my arms. I did my best as well to keep it in me—to replicate the brush of every inch—so that when not on my way or treading I could read it brightly in my mind.

[The door into the man's front hallway had a lock as large as my whole hand. The lock was darkly tarnished, as if it'd smoldered in a fire. It had numbers scratched into it, shining slits cut in the smudge. The lock jostled in its turning—it would pop a little, kind of moan. If you touched it in the right condition, and applied a certain pressure, the house would open up.]

[The door, when stubborn, made my teeth ache.]

[The door's color could change.]

[This door would also sometimes appear inside my household, in a place I will not name.

[*Why hello.*]]]

[The thing about the moving, then, inside the other house is this: there I began to feel alive. I mean coming through the door even that first time, I felt eruption in my hair. I felt an ocean, or something liquid, flushing through the insides of my skin, around my abdomen or womb. A gush or warming throb. I would admit to sensual elaborations but I can't be sure that this was that. As you know or may have heard there are often not the words for sorts of things in which you feel as if something about you is not the same, or if it might be in the midst of shifting, or. The floor in the hallway inside the front door was dark and made of wood. It had a seamless finish. *See?* I could slither on it. I could be. The hall's walls were also seamless and hung with photos of faceless men. By faceless I mean their fronts were facing backwards, away from the camera, from me. It was not certain what they'd been made to look at, what they wanted, who they'd need.

[No one came to see.]]]

[In the air between our houses, washed in that off-light, I moved head-on into the sludge, into the crap that sluiced the sidewalks, most everything knee-deep.

    [I came up the hill to where a children's school bus had derailed, dodging the curve that still loomed bright across the street, its blurby blip having shrunk some in the last weeks but still looming large enough to gulp a head. I concretely came to the location all the birds at the same moment had flew into the same small spot. Where all the rock had turned to cola. Where the air barfed neon breathing. Where if you'd had the right hands and the right eyes, you could reach up in the sky and press a button. *I won't say who or when or what the button did or how often.*

[In the wrought red sheen across this section, I could not unknot my tongue.]]

[I came down the hill on the other side towards where you used to see the mile-wide shopping mall, most of the stores already run under with fungus so deep black they said you could name it from the moon—not that we knew the moon here anymore, that same fungus having clogged it also out, and how the heat had cracked our telescopes. I walked unblinking, cragged with tremor. I was following my legs. I grew a little roasted in the sunning. The air seemed to want to spit me out. It stung in fury the more I waddled, the further out I ever got, though I never felt my eyes go blink. No blink. I could not stop. I walked. I walked. I walked. I walked. I walked. I walked. I walked. I walked straight on into that yawning. I walked head-on into the rip that ruined the birds and ate the buildings and found myself for a long time cradled only in that light. I walked.

[In that light the bevel dawning.]

[In that light some running crud.]

[In that light a hundred windows of someone, wherever, what.

[That light, my body, stretched to all ends.]]]

[In that light I felt the floor.]]

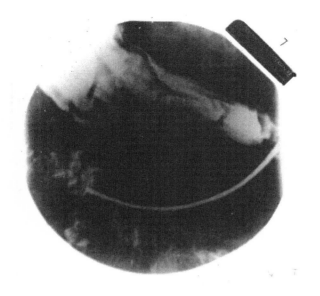

[In the light I made a bargain. I shook hands inside myself. My sternum slurred and veins culled open. My elbows grew into my hands. Then the hands were all around me, their nails slick as the night. Palms big as my belly. Fingerprints as blank as _____.]

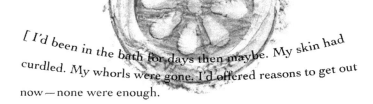

[I'd been in the bath for days then maybe. My skin had curdled. My whorls were gone. I'd offered reasons to get out now — none were enough.

[My back was numb and I was clean.]]

[I'd read the same thing four times hardly blinking. A book my mother'd found when I was small — found fit in the crack cut in her ceiling, on the other side of which was mud. Our house had gotten buried briefly. My father'd gotten swallowed in the midst of shoveling it off. All those old nights she'd spread beside me, writhed in reciting, her weird body humped and lumped and ragged — her voice still endless in my head now — a kind of drill or gum or gun.

[I could read now without reading.

[I did not have to think of me.]]

[I was in the room then, I was sitting. I felt another kind of rub. The ceiling seemed hung nearer. The tub began to groan.

[Inside the room the tub grew longer, downward, an eggshell crackle in my trust. I heard ripping. I saw snow men.]

[My lungs began to bust.]

[My hair stuck on the tub slope and caught and tugged taut to my scalp. Warm bathwater sloshed my nostrils. Bubbles stung my eyes with color. There was so much unasked steam.]

[I put my hands against the stretching. My nails slunk on the sheen.]

[By the time the tub had quit increasing, my bathroom was the sky.]

[From where I was I saw no handholds—no exit method, no good go. This was where I'd be now. The wet was cold and I was nude. My skin gleamed from old lather. My body, plump as ever—rung with soft-stitched patterns of grown-out glow. My bag of belly with no baby. My titties stung. My hair knotted full of where I'd been once—or been maybe—or been—or been.]

[One place I'd been for sure once was a circus. There were clowns and crowds and wicked light. There was a bear. I'll be specific: my head got caught on fire.

　　[Yes it did.]]

　[Yes I had been to a circus. Yes.]]

38

[I had been once to a sea. Of this much I am certain, no condition. There was something on the waves. I stood out in the waves. I stood up on the foamed flat sea head and watched where it touched me, where it went.

[I could not see the other end of the ocean, or the bottom— *where it went* I guess is what I mean.]

[Shit.

[Say—]]]

[I also could remember I'd been meant once to wed some little man I'd found through lengths of wire—our years of archived correspondence now wiped away by heat or spore—our machines bumped to dust. In the absence of all this other we agreed to meet waist-high in the muck of streets and struts and food rooms and all else. This man was someone even then. He had such stuff behind his eyes, such malls. He had my father's sense of timing, his puffed brush of beard, his locking. Among the flies and splotch and lupus we helped keep each other clean. We danced on rubble. We made tremble. We tried at last to feel just fine.

[A week after, he shared the same scratched lather that'd filled my mother. My mother who could speak every sentence all at once—who could become, some nights, my father, and we would lean.

[This man, I saw his headstone daily even after—
even slept there sometimes, while I could—until
the muck consumed that also, under—and still I
kept on to that spot—my best-guessed landmark,
his skin a kind of rind on the dried crud most
above where he lay buried crusted over—until
that also piled higher—layers layered—layers
brined so high there was hardly room to stand
between the crusting and the sky.]

[He hung in memory awhile after till that joined
blackened with the blur—and then again I sat in
small rooms—and then again I was alone.]]

[I'd had other husbands also, maybe—I'd learned
and ate my ticking list: George, Jan, G., T., Tony,
Rick, Ron, Walker, Everett, Louis, Luis, B., Bryan,
Robert, Rosen, Lot, Luellen, Loice, Alfonso, Rob,
Bob, Bobby, H.D., I.—as well as the ones I'll never
mention and the ones I never gave a name.]

[It's impolite to sit outside a burning building—even if
that fucked and burning building is the only one still on
the block.]]

[I stood in the bathwater. I wasn't sure which way to
move. I had the book still, clenched white-knuckled. I
couldn't think of where to sit it. The soap dish was high
up with my shampoos and control knobs. All I saw was
slick and flat, soap-spotted.

[I held the book against my chest. I held it longer. I felt its weight begin to age. It felt unbearable, this condition. I set the book down soft on lukewarm water. It stayed afloat a minute before its covers bulged and it sank under the lip.

  [The words were there inside my head still. Some words were — BLOISSIS OINGE BINBASSUM LER MIT OINTSIN LESH KERR NUM. Some words had spurs or burped incisions. Some words sounded like things I'd said myself.

    [TRUE or FALSE:
    The best-licked words I will not share.]]]

[Some weeks, I should mention, I would live off candy bars. There was a lot you could have by wanting. There were several miles of untamed air. When birds weren't swooping at my skull and hair with their cracked beaks while they still could, they'd sing awful hymns like records ripped, as if they'd never seen a sun. The birds could make words also. They had patterns in their pupils. I patched the larger holes in my rooftop with the fattest glass that I could carry. Nearly everything was gleam — it'd rained windshields and coffee table tops for several days — and I would shine. I'd stand in the bathroom mirror for endless hours brushing my teeth in one long stroke. *Once the weight gets into your elbow, that's when it's nicest. Nothing like pressure to help remind.* When I spit the spit out, it was often colored. When I rinsed the sink, it took a while. Sometimes I had to use my fingers to help the water sluice away what I'd asked out of me by force.]]

41

[From here, way down inside the tub, I learned to see the tub itself. The weird lacquered lines of years of run and rinsing, my mother neck-deep, awaiting drown, hoping she might soak the syndrome from her skin's lens—or that the tub might suck off her disease. The hair grown on her stomach and eyelids, on her back, went soft and slushy in the washing. Her sores were smaller underwater. From above they looked like homes.

[Along the elongation now the walls showed long glossed spots of darker colors, birthmarks transferred from a leg—or burns or bruises—the striations of smaller spores embedded in the grain. Even the soap— our cleansing slivers—had left its chalky whitewashed zones of foam.]

[I'd sat so long soaked in this slather—so long trying to get rid of something else.]

[I put my tongue against the tub now—I could discern several things.

[
1. This is my mother's flavor.
2. This is Comet cleanser.
3. This is me.
]]]

[I could hear the room above me moving—something in
it—someone. I could hear them there inside me, also
echoed, jostling around. They were moving things and
using hammers, screws and scissors, saws with teeth. An
all-purpose sound of some undoing. The air was stuffed
with grunts. Grinding from my bedroom. There was
much they could break—the music box I'd drifted off to
as an infant and ever since then, one night after another,
the gray gears having churned so long alongside one
another the song was wholly new from what it'd been,
but still—I couldn't sleep without it whirring, its runny
guggle—oh I'd tried. I'd wormed through endless nights
in old motels on strange vacations in strange air, blinking
straight on until light, my teeth grinding in its absence,
an ill replacement, ached—

[The ceramic mask my mother had worn for bedtime,
preferring her face covered in case of passersby—
though I assured her no one ever would—she was
always smelling men—]

[The photographs I'd taken—paper money, though
now these days, hell, okay—]

[Who am I kidding—what could matter—what could
be wanted of me now—what that hasn't been already
had so often over—]

[and yet I've never sickened—not for any.

[Take the lot.

43

[TRUE or FALSE:
More than stealing, I was afraid of what might be
left behind—
a hope or reason, new directions—more fodder
for this sorry sore.]]]]

[The noise went on for hours. I heard windows. I think
birds. Machines were ushered in at some point—I could
hear the gearshift and the churn—I could hear the
collapsing in the men's breath—there were men up there,
I am sure. They never spoke, or not loud enough for me
to hear. They were really working hard, I think. I think
they thought I would have fought them. No matter how I
moved or thought or angled shouting I could not signal
their attention. I used every phrase I'd learned. I called
their names out from my list. I—

[No. They did not have names yet.

[No they didn't.]

[No.]]

[The air vents sighed. The tub was cold. I'd gone past
numb and into neon. The shaking started in my legs
first where the water touched the most, then moved
through me to freeze the loudest in certain sectors of
my head. My brain adhered against my skull. I heard a
hundred termites, heard an error—my teeth electric
side by side.

[I shook so hard my skin was peeling. I loosened it around my gut. I watched it come up from my tummy, along my abdomen in loops, the flesh beneath a little brighter, my hair consumed with speech.

　　[My skin pooled in the bathwater, sizzling a little, sinking in.]]

[In the tub enamel I saw my reflection and I smeared it with my thumb.]]]

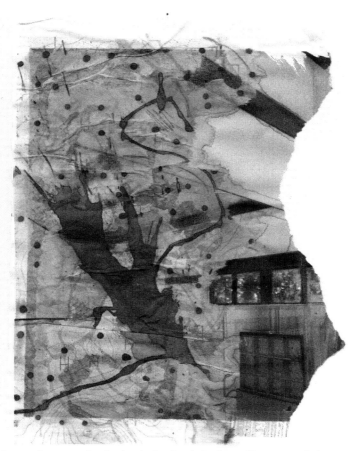

[At my feet now in the bath the book had swollen several times—
so large it filled the whole blank basin—it sponged around my
knees. The pages slathered on my soft legs, unshaven, the pages,
even wet, erupting cuts. It swelled also in me, cloned in my colon,

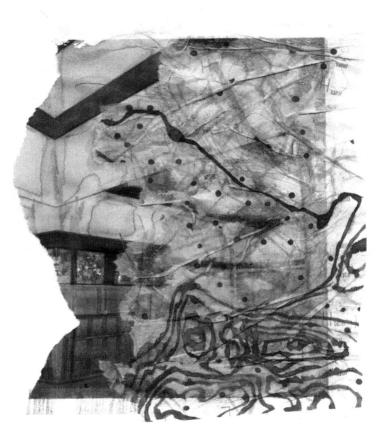

head, intestines—the text on the battered pages made so
large now swimming in me—it grabbed my hands—it
pressed my sides and chest and back together.

[There was a pocket around my mouth where I could inhale and another keyhole above, where though the noise had begun to quiet I still sensed the others' lurk.]

[I tried to move among the blubbered book in ways.

  [I found my blood—my breathing—in the book.

    [I found—I found—]]]

[I squirmed. The book was pressing. I forced my feet above my head. I could not sleep. My eyes stayed open. My body purpled in this drivel. My endless seeping spit corralled around me—here in the smudged tub where my mom had washed me as a young one and later, both much older, I'd washed her, our skins the same. I used my nails to rip small motions through the paper— through this bloated noxious book— till after some long moments, I was looking at my face—looking right there at my own face!—my minor me therein reflected—*old*. This time at once not only in the book but in the spotless mirrored lid that clogged the drain.

  [This time, in such position, I was someone that I knew. I had those holes still. I was smiling. My head had sweated white.

    [My head had several hundred heads.]]]

[With its rusty chain clenched in fat fingers, I pulled the lid up off the drain.]]

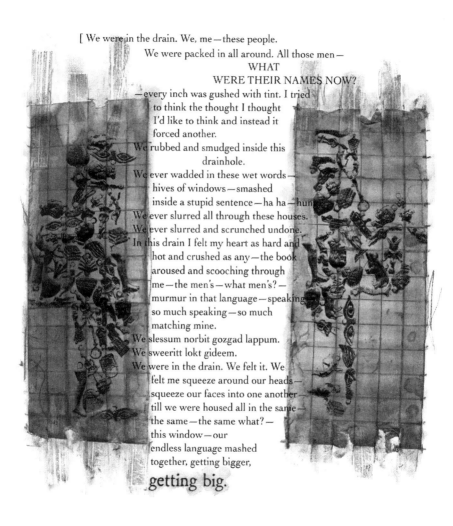

[We were in the drain. We, me—these people.
We were packed in all around. All those men—
WHAT
WERE THEIR NAMES NOW?
—every inch was gushed with tint. I tried
to think the thought I thought
I'd like to think and instead it
forced another.
We rubbed and smudged inside this
drainhole.
We ever wadded in these wet words—
hives of windows—smashed
inside a stupid sentence—ha ha—hun
We ever slurred all through these houses.
We ever slurred and scrunched undone.
In this drain I felt my heart as hard and
hot and crushed as any—the book
aroused and scooching through
me—the men's—what men's?—
murmur in that language—speaking
so much speaking—so much
matching mine.
We slessum norbit gozgad lappum.
We sweeritt lokt gideem.
We were in the drain. We felt it. We
felt me squeeze around our heads—
squeeze our faces into one another—
till we were housed all in the same—
the same—the same what?—
this window—our
endless language mashed
together, getting bigger,
getting big.

49

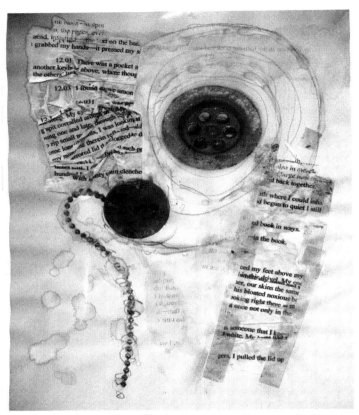

[From the drain, from off wherever, we—I—smooshed into a room. This room was minute or it was massive, full of sunning like a hive. The walls had many tiny pictures—*I will not describe them with these words.* My arms poured their blood to one another back and forth. My warmth increased at a rate concurrent to the room's needs. My head began to boil. I said goodbye to certain things. I slushed myself into the color.

[The next room I knew was baby blue—blue as in the way the oceans nestled down to just one fat lather—blue like the nipples of the dead cow my dad drug in from the street before the light lit, each too big to fit a mouth on, but so rich—blue like where I pinched myself thin to keep warm through the evenings, only—blue like the abdomen of all the moths I'd swallowed in my sleep.]

[The next room I knew was rubbed red like an eraser to the chest—like the zap of something with a thorax—like where the teeth split and let such blood.]

[The next room was not quite there but I was in it.]

[The next room was bronzed and it was burring and I could taste it in my mouth. The taste was like the way the crux of my elbow had with all its season and its spit— how I could suck that notch for hours and imagine who it was—who I was—*where the bells rung is another notion in itself.*]

[The next room had been turned over and gone hazy at the edges, as if it were several rooms at once, embedded. The walls sloped in rash directions. The ceiling bled to chunked gunk on the carpet. The gunk stayed on my hands thereafter. In each room beyond this one I left a little where I touched, some of me coming off with it, my itch, my stench, my cells.]

[The next room was wrong and paling—the way my skin would go in teenage winter—and then later, all year-round—days when the doors locked and I could not get them open even when I hadn't tried.]

[The next room was made of wobble. Magnetic tape streaming from the rafters, bifurcating blonde split-ends. Cashed.]

[The next room hung stuffed with smoke and lather, leather dripping from the seams, and the skin of children shucked for ransom, inches of organs rendered clean — skin of anyone who'd been kissed by anyone in the mental weeks of me.]

[The next room was cordoned in the corners a prism, and thus held many angles, splayed around. There were all the colors of the rooms I'd seen before, as well as rooms to come—which I could not have sensed yet, and I did—the minor mansions, rooms waiting that I would come in and get old. Through the lining of the prism I could see a woman in a kitchen doing something with her teeth. She got bigger when she knelt down. She was—]

[The next room was made of charcoal, glowing embers, wretched rock. I'd seen this sort of fissure elsewhere. It resembled our front yard—though my father was not out in the yard now digging with his fingers, nor my mother with her mossy hair up, screeching at his back. My little brother was not buried where the pets were. Through little holes some women sang—words I knew a little, volumed in my veins. If I looked closely, though it burned, I could see into those women's open mouths— their curling tongues all caked with resin, their rotted tonsils—what they'd eaten, who they drank.]

[The next room was every person and their aura(s) and their shit. *I almost stayed forever in this room*.]

[The next room was none of the above.]

[The next room was stained with thrumming, beaten awful, seeping up with cruddy flesh, splashed in the seep of acid from certain stomachs, inches we'd hidden in our years.]

[The next room was melon yellow, zapped with lightning—huge bananas—bumblebees—bees runned with honey—their own honey—bees eating bees—up to my neck and in my knees.]

[The next room had a tiny doorman who murmured in my ear.]]

O SKUM   LUMM-

-ED EEP-NIT, HOSSLORE

[The next room was lined with shelves so high I could not see. Some soft choir overhead. Stink of paper rot. I had on a dress that had burned once in a fire. I had black hair on my hands. I moved along the books touching a couple—leather, skin. When I touched the books they read themselves aloud. Once the books began they would not cease.

   [The books had many voices. One book said—
   OISKUM   LO   LUMM-ED   EEP-NIT,
   HOSSLOREFEING LINGZUMP BEED. One book
   just said my name over and over. One book would not
   come open. In one book there was a child's picture, and
   a child inside the child, each made of teeth.]

   [One book opened me instead.]

   [One book became a door.]]

[This next room I'd been into—this room knew I knew.
In this room I'd been a child awhile. I'd wet the bed for
years. Some evenings I would float and spray like hoses.
After that I took to bleeding. I'd slept on the bed until I
couldn't stand the spores, then I began to sleep around it,
or inside. The room remained the same no matter what I
wanted. The bed was always there.

   [This same bed now—in this small room, down the
   drain—this bed was warped with ropes and folds of
   mold—glossed green sheets of spiny likeness,
   burrowed, mud-caked, and bouqueted, like the yard.

   [I was breathing. I breathed into the bed. I breathed
   the bed.]

[I breathed.]]

[The walls — the ceiling, bookcase, closet, clothing — all had also grown a little rind. It lined my lungs with each inhaling. I heard the insects nuzzled in, around.]

[I could hear — I think so — somewhere — could feel my mother's massive crinkled lungs. At first her voice came from the headboard. She was there inside the wood. Then she was an awning up above us. Then she rustled crooked in my toes. And in the crinkle of my linings.

[Her voice said many things.

[Her voice spoke that silent language. At first just at my ear, then all around. Her voice a fountain spurting over. Quaking grease between my teeth.]]

[She became the room, my mother.

[*There she is.*]]

[My head turned to the side to be hit.]

[My eyes clenched and blinked and looked again.]]]

[In the room now there were several of me standing. There was me and me and me. So many kinds I could not remember, slabs of skin I'd long abandoned.

[There was my awkward version, age 13, the year I'd looked more like a man than ever—my features flat and cracked and rashy, a crappy mustache for my lip—that coal black hair grown in my ears and eyelids, combing over. This was the me who felt afraid she'd live forever. This was the me who slept for weeks unmoved. This me now stood against the wall and looked into my eyes with my own eyes.]

[There was my version, 18, that year of no dawns, that year the sea became a solid, that year the walls and ants and trees somehow grew teeth—this silent, skinny me emerging through the mossy carpet from just the neck up, mouthing more words I could not hear.]

[There was my version not-quite-a-year-yet, rolled on the ground nude and coocooing—lips all chapped and bubbled over with a sort of spit that bulbed like glass—a wash of markings on my belly—legions in my hair.]

[All my other versions—I couldn't count them—some were so ugly—they swarmed around—standing, squatting, hung from the ceiling, eating dinner, spinning, touched—I could not look at most of them directly.]

[I could not look.]]

[One of me began to speak.

[I did not know which one of me this one was.]]

69

[The voice came in perpendicular to my mother's, at first clashing—the walls began to bend—then the two voices joined together. The two voices formed another voice, this one numbing, humming out.]]

[The room then took to turning inward. We all were also walking. We had to move out of my way. Another of me was speaking also. And another. Heads full of breath and cold lawnmowers. The house had walls and halls.

[And another voice. Another. We were we, where, we were one(s).]]

[The room had shook. The walls were nowhere. The walls erupted blisters from their sweat. There was this voice. There was this nowhere.]

[The voice was speaking louder.]
[The voice was speaking.]
[Saying something.]

[This voice was speaking louder.]

[It was speaking louder.]

[It was loud.]

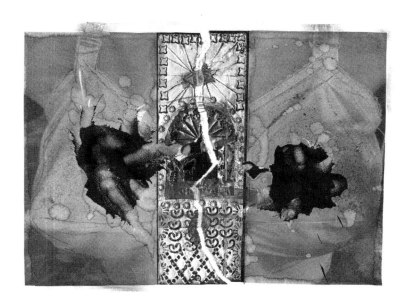

[In the room then I could not see the sentence. I felt a presence in me worming, making meat. There was a sense I could not scratch, no matter which way or how about it. I heard my body near me turning, turned. I was old as I could be.

[Old as anybody ever.]

[The room began to gleam.]

[When I looked again, then, there I was—my slivered visage staring at me on the backside of the bathroom door. My bathroom, same as ever—I'd hung the mirror there myself—found it laying face up in a field down from my house once, glown hot and rotted with the sun. It burned my fingers as I pried it, marred my cheek, my chest, my sternum as I lumbered it back into my home.

  [The mirror's face now had cracked right down the center.]

  [I could not hear the men still in other rooms.]]

[From the tub I saw my bed still sitting silent, covers made, unwrinkled, in need of wash.

  [The ceiling fan above the mattress spun so fast it made a clicking, the way it always had and did and would forever.

  [*What was it about the clicking?*]]]

[The mirror in its ruining corralled my face in two soft halves. It split my tits, my neck and belly. It fit deeper than the door. If I moved a little to this or that side I could make one half or the other that much bigger. I could make my eyes not there.]

[My legs were numb still. I couldn't stand up. I could move my arms, though. I could move them.]

[I touched my face. I felt my face.]

  [I touched the room.]]]

72

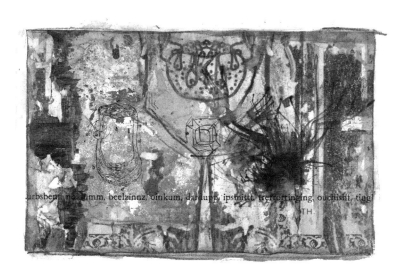

[I found myself inside my sofa. Found I'd squeezed my skin between the crease—hot in the act of reclaiming all the crap the cushions'd eaten: my change, my pens, my mother's mask. There was more there then than ever. I could see into the dark. *This was mine. And this was mine.*

    [These were wet weeks. These were worse ones—I'd begun to taste my age. Whereas before my mode had been all smother, now something in me wanted more. My brain would worm in terms of hurting: how much could I make?]]

[There was new knock. The sofa shook some.

[The house stretched in several ways—and/or held someone wanting and/or somewhere. I felt a movement in my skin. I couldn't keep from thinking—*if this could be that man come back—or if it could—or could—or if.*]]

[I came from the sofa alive for life forever, flexed for throbbing. My teeth had learned a little greed.]

[At the door I pressed my head against the eye. I looked and looked and saw and there was nothing—yet not quite the kind of nothing now expected—the front yard spooled with break; the piles of glass the sky had barfed, the graying grass where in ancient summers I'd rolled around and rashed, played dead, where I'd stay still for hours hardly nodding till the ants found and made tunnels of my nostrils—I mean the yard now was *nothing* nothing—I mean just color—hell, not even—smudge. The yard, I guess, had been deleted, like another stupid line.

  [Likely I should not have touched the door.]

  [Likely that would have been the wise thing— though there was so much that I wanted.]]

  [I pulled the knob with both arms buzzing, some kind of somewhere, turning the page in a massive book.]]

[Behind the door was no man standing—no special offer—none at all. The gap instead was filled with bubble. The bubble invited itself in. It moved in sound of exhale—*whose breath where?—what lungs?* I huddled backwards, calmly nodding, while the bubble grew and grew into the house, into my tongue.

[This balloon, rendered in ex-fat, hid with the eyelids of the gone, stitched with the names I tried to hide around me, the names of who or who and who.]]

[Pressed in the corner, through the window, I saw the balloon stretched and writhing over all. It'd wrapped around the neighbor's roof and porch—it'd wrapped around the children in the yard—*if there were children out there any longer*—it'd wrapped around the sideways trees and breeze and sky tines and the plasticine arch where we'd erupted and been stitched. What other things it'd wrapped I could somehow name and not quite name.

[*Lurbsbent, noidumm, beelzinnz, oinkum, dardupp, ipsmittt, trerrorringing, ouchisht, tigglebda, squee... ...*]]

[Inside the house my sore skin flexed against the old paint. My groggy skull complexed and pressured on the spackled boards that aligned my light. There wasn't time to be displeased. The balloon, bright pinked and endless, pressed to the divots in my nose—the entry to my brain holes—it screeched against my teeth. My throat had stretched a little, whining for my lungs.

[In my gums I heard the bell.]]]]

[And so now then as the pruned balloon that'd rapped the front door and wobbled in, replete—this fat and fucked thing that'd learned to stretch forever and had filled the downstairs end to end—*what downstairs, motherfucker? this awful home is all one room*—in the sudden silence I heard nothing but the rubber wanting more—some hover—and in the weird sheen of the stretching I felt a bubble in the oven of my chest—and I waited patiently for nowhere—and I was not afraid—

   [I lay gummed up in the grunting, my skin against my skin. My mouth filled with old aromas of my stomach, in my goo.]

   [My eyes could pop. My spine would listen. My knees kept turning into oil. The house and I. The yard, the crud and I. Our burn. Our, um—]]

[As I began in recognition of the way the seam had split apart, the way each eyelid hid an eon, the balloon desisted in its rumble. I and the altogether lidless surface, gushed with foreign air—such false air that'd spread to fill my home around me—ours—both of us sandwiched, scraping somewhat—our plastic moment stopped.

   [This swelling knew the room then—it held the room—was the room itself—and other rooms compiled—]

[This swelling slid. It huffed and swished away as pustule, like what in all those younger years I'd tried to kill about my face. I watched the rubber pucker. I kicked its deflate. I bit it on. As a soft and gummy puddle, it slithered back out through the door.]]

[And now the thing was headed elsewhere — also leaving. Fine.]

[Whichever way — my head was gone.]]]

And this was mine

[Through the window the neighbor's home stood a little crooked, slightly smeared and smashed among returning light.

[In the long contusion of the room's glue I felt my innards going slush—wanting ways out of myself itself—my skin goosefleshed and mostly smothered bright where rubber'd rubbed—and scored with fields of tiny potholes where my arm's soft follicles had been ripped out by the root.]

[Again the house was empty with furniture rearranged in place—the blades of the ceiling fan busted off from where the pressure had bent them backwards.]]

[I was standing in the house.]

[A sense of time passed, and light flexed all over in and out around me, glossing my hair and upper body, kissing off and curling walls—the circumference of my pupils shrinking, swelling, shrinking, on.]

[The front door still stood wide open. I couldn't think of what to do. I did not move, though not for trying, and not for not trying wholly either.]

[I was there.]]

[Again the front door closed and came again, the hinges hung and bumped with rust—though I'd cleaned them with my teeth, a dinner. Outside the air just stood there standing—kind of colored, though through the spy-hole I could see the outside still again. In the yard instead of mold or bubble, there were people. People people— packed in so tight into the front yard that I could not see around them—not the grass or sky or sun or street or mud or sleep surrounding. I could not see the rashed horizon that had in recent years turned on its side and slid and made a bruise, had still given me some small sentence of strange comfort, knowing it at least had stuck around.

[These people all had eyes for me. They were looking. Their lids would flitter, run with ripple. There were men and women and upright babies, some in the forms of dogs and ants and bulls and aphids, but all still built to fill a bed. There were those in business suits and those in jumpers and some in zipper-pants or hockey jerseys or tattered gowns of many colors. Some bodies were ones I recognized a little, perhaps encased somewhere on undeveloped film, or perhaps my mother or my father rearranged, or some of my versions the other room had held, or those we'd put into the ground forgotten, and those I'd called upon in silence and in begging—all of these now pressed together, many- skinned. We stood and looked together at us all.]

[Overhead the night was white and full.]

[Overhead the night had opened and all throughout it I saw words. Words made of skin or spit or coffee.

[The words were saying something.]

80

[I heard myself begin to speak—

    [*And this was mine*, I said, my voice enormous, all-vibrating. *And this was mine. And this was mine.*]]]

[And now my words continued on into the overhead, joining the others. And when I paused again the people blinked, their size now billowing around them, the fat of their backs and foreheads spurting skyward, spreading to fill up one and another over all.]

[Inside my own mouth I felt a sputter, a collapsing.]]

[Inside the house I turned away.]

[I turned and saw the room the way I'd seen it endless times, and yet as I saw it again I became aware of something different in its walls. The house for years had held a hundred clocks though now the silence licked my neck. The roof had once been see-through though now it reflected me back in it. And though the carpet down the hallway still led back to where most evenings I would sleep—*if I didn't conk out by the window, by the oven, in search of stairs—stairs to somewhere, over, ever*—I found then as I moved into the room to stand inside the room, the room around began to breathe—and where once the space had puckered and grown small and made a place where I could wallow, instead inside the room now the walls kept going. The walls went long and painted paisley, inlaid with words I could not read. Words not on the sky or on my tongue or elsewhere in me. Also, the smell of something, antiseptic, or new air, though I could not breathe the feature. I saw a minor wash of light. Somewhere longways in that light I saw certain shapes that as I moved my eyes to define then also spread apart. The air was pixilated. There were skin cells.]

81

[The walls went further on.]

[The walls could shift in size, I found.]

[I spun inside my head. I tried not to look or blink. I felt tired beyond ill. I thought of how I'd had my head in other years and where my tongue was. I thought of the center of the earth—of the center of the center of the earth—of the center of my mind. I thought of those I'd seen only in pictures—*how everywhere could be another—when this end could be an end.*

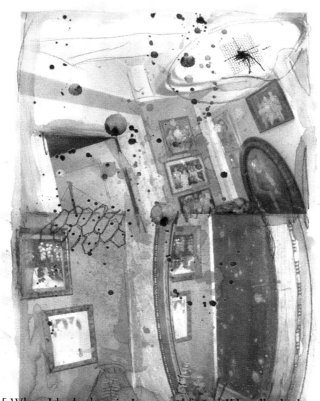

[When I looked again I saw and found I'd walked a long way in my thoughts. These walls now were painted red, whereas before the house's walls had only ever been blank — *though some years we'd tried to paint it and the paint would sink in or slip off* — as surface in which certain things could hide — *such as,* my mother once had written on a note she'd made me eat: *insects, churches, names and numbers, women, ideas, liquid, lust.*

83

[Just down the hall from where I stood now not quite shaking, I saw another little room. The room had other walls mostly the color of old teeth and another mirror and no window.

  [The room was somewhere that I'd been, I knew, or somewhere at least that had been in me.

    [In the room I saw my mother sitting sideways on a stool. This mother's face was not smushed and runny the way it had been when she went under. Her lips were not quadrupled with disease. Her hair, though, had been pulled down tight against her head so that her skin stretched and glinted in the light. In the tub beside her she'd run a bath. With her left hand she stirred the water, keeping the surface wrong for dust.]

    [My mother motioned for me to come toward her, to climb in and wash myself. Her hand curled the air around it, set it glowing. My mother did not blink.

    [I moved my mouth to say something I'd had inside for some long time—*another thing I'd never gotten out, mazed inside my endless mouth*—instead hot water spouted out, warm, a fountain, splashing down against the ground. *The bathwater in my me.*]]

[I lived then in that moment the same day over and over for eons until I returned to the age where I'd begun. My mother was no longer there.]

[There was so much else left to admire.

  [There was so much light inside me that I could no longer even see.]]

84

[I turned to face the room.]

[By the time I'd crossed the room halfway again I was 99 years old. My forearms runned with wrinkles. My fat was hanging down. I weighed now something near 280 lbs., whereas when I'd left the water I was small. Small like an idea, like every hour. The new weight woke in me, a tumor. I could feel some piglets rutting. My feet refused to leave the floor. I thought to turn to see myself in something shined. The room still contained a few—window glass; I'd left a spoon out; in the light the table gleamed. For several years this room had blackened any mirror—this room, which now refused to end. I thought to think to stop but I kept going with some indication of my reflection or some reflection I'd contained.

[In the room I crossed the room halfway again.

[I crossed the room halfway again.

[I crossed the room halfway again.

[I crossed the room halfway again.

[I crossed the room halfway again.]]]]]

[After several hours in the light, I came to a room that held
a bed. The light had made me tired. I no longer felt my
arms—or felt them only slightly, filled with buzzing, lined
with hives—and in each hive another person, or a window. I
sat down on the bed. I flexed back on the mattress with my
arms limp at my sides. My arms eating their muscles. From
on my side the room was small. The room was smaller then.
The room was made of meat.

87

[The room spread through itself, still shrinking—and came out the other side.]]]

[The room was many rooms I no longer could contain.

[This certain room was filled with liquid. In this liquid there was light—shone from the stubbled ceiling wrought with scratching—illegible, duressed.

[Deeper down the liquid's thickness ate the glow and scrunched the space to gone. Perhaps still somewhere in there, drowned: my bed, my bedside table, my sleeping gown, my sleep itself, my head etched in the dresser mirror.

[Sometimes, in night, this room would boil.]]

[Sometimes the wet would flood with fungus, stuffed so tight you couldn't see—fungus like what'd grown over the forest—fungus like our sea—fungus like that covering my mother in her fragments and my father gone wherever.

[The fungus grew in several colors. Inside the fungus nits would burrow. Their paths would cause a pattern in which one might decipher incantation, tired verse.]]

[In this room for years I'd hid a cat named mine until I woke to find how she'd combusted.]]]

[This certain room sat flush in fat. Chunks I'd known once. Shedded pounds—made of the shit I ate and carried with me, never needing. Even further hidden light.]

[This certain room held certain people, mashing in and outside of the house, and me here both within and hung above. Folks I might have known once. At least one, but much as hundreds, maybe. Listen—it was impossible to count. They formed a throng, these people, became each other. There wasn't anywhere to go. Their eyes would toddle, sloshing, all one body. Their foreheads distended with the beat. They did not flinch when the house caught fire, nor for my shouting, nor when their air became a gong.]

[Upwards in my room of windows, I held my breath to stop the fog. This certain room was wide as nighttime, wide as all of where I'd been. This room could hold a house within this house already. This room would warm towards its center. Inside this certain room I'd sweat and sweat and sweat. *What years of rain my body gave.*]

89

[In this room of windows I'd somehow gotten stuck. I'd come into it through some long hall—not like birth or death or dying—though I'd heard my mother's voice. The hall branched to halls and halls again—halls sunk slick with bubbling from where the light had made the house melt—from where the house mashed against itself like clockwork without clocks. I'd gotten crud all on my skirt—black thick motor crud clogged in my fingers, hair. I felt it want to flex around me. It slithered up my thigh. Only by rolling in the light and holding my eyes shut and fists clasped and shouting out every word I thought I knew, I kept the crud and what it wanted out of my inside at least a while.

  [This room of windows did not have a door. As if I'd been inside it there forever. As if I'd—if I'd—if I'd—if—

    [However more I fought to remember, the more I buckled—deeper white.]]]

[I turned to try to see my face reflected in the room's glass, though no matter how I turned the surface curved obscure. I could not make the light behave around me. I could not find my reflected eyes—though I felt them with my fingers—my eyes right there in my head—eyes all wet and kind of greenish—green from my mother, whose glassy glare was somewhere else. I had a picture of her somewhere. *Can you see it? Can you see the picture?*

  [*Try again.*]

90

[In my lap, one small forgiveness, the tape recorder hummed. Such speech spurred from its speaker. My voice did not quite sound mine—more like a man I'd met one night, I think. There'd been a man, yes, then, outside my own voice—my voice—mine. My voice, a tremored version, blabbing. I'd always hated my own sounds. I only recognized myself in the certain phrasings, rasps and inflections, flicks of tongue taught by disease. The language chopped in and out a little where the tape went wet or warped, and those were what parts I liked best.]

[On tape I spoke a stutter-language, barked.]

[I said: YUNYI-DEEKLETOTISH EISBEN BEELVIT NOIKKID DISHDOR. LER MANNIFIFS. PEEB BEWEREROIT CHACHERRERUM NOIVAT BEERY, BELVEIT SMART. SMART TOIFFINTZIT, QER-QA WATTLE WETTED WINTZ-CHOLD CHAH.]

[I did not know why I was saying that.]

[The tape went on in that same fashion for several hours. When it reached the end of one side, it flipped over to the other and went on. It could have gone on forever in this manner. The machine had burst its batteries to gunk. My voice fixed me transfixed a little.]

[I played the tape again, again.]]

[From inside the room of windows, there were things that I could see, such as the rooms. The things I saw out through the windows, unlike most windows would often shift.

[For certain lengths, through certain windows, when there were not rooms, there'd be color—sheaths of long flat blue or white, like televisions. Other times the glass showed water: condensation budding on the outside— someone other breathing?—oceans, torrents, sideways rain. Sometimes the water shot so strong it looked like nothing. Sometimes the path of the dripping traced out names.

[Through other windows at other hours I saw whole long yards of crumpled trees. I saw the dirt upturned and goring, blasted black around the edges—babies bloated in the sinkholes where old buildings had once stood—now uplifted or sunk in or crumbling. I saw gobs of gush from milking candles slopping wax against the coast, burbling at the mushy sandlots where as children we'd dug and buried, where we'd traced our names and watched them wash, where we whispered of replication.

[I saw rabbits, black wheels, bunting, massive nests of broiling breast, chicken wire, foreheads, long strips of skin culled from underground—all of this packed into a single pixel, pulling the sky down—another minor speckle on the grief.]]

[At other times there were hours where disease would grease the sun. A pocky blob which made the light skitch. An umbrella in my sinus. At certain angles the lighting made the room of windows stretch down deeper than itself. During these conditions I would lay flat as ever, if I could manage, and press my hands against my lungs—I would listen to me churning as my voice went on in spiral. At times I'd find myself repeating what the tape said, the way it said it. I chimed in right along.]

[In one window, for a minute, I saw the pasty bump of someone's womb.]

[Another time, a blinking iris, wide as awnings, green as mine.]]

[One thing I could not see through the windows was the outside of the house—at least any walls or roofs or grass or driveways or the yard, or any of those other things one might find when looking inward from the outside, even now.]

[Through the windows there was sound. It came not clear from one direction, but moved if and by its will. It came not clear from one direction, but from one ear to the other and up the middle, and through my numbing gums and cell walls. As a small child I'd been burned once standing close to an explosion—my father's chemist visions in the closet, mixing crap of several sorts together—trying, he claimed, to make medication that'd take the fungus off his skin—off the backyard— off the sky—even since then, in all those wormed years, I'd never learned the way of the vibration. In the night I'd hear men cough, hear them whisper to me. I'd hear livestock stuck in my bonnet; rodents swelling in the pipes while drowning. There were often long low bowed tones. Muted trumpets. Baby goggle. Mewing of a horse.

[Now, by sure, I knew, though—the house had learned a song.]

[The song could slither in one ear and out the other, or it could hover in my back, or it could fill my entire stomach with more ballooning—*did you know each inch goes on forever?*—or it could hush me into a tent of awful silence, where I knew nothing but my gut. Whichever way it came, it came on. It flossed me like a dentist and swiped the smacky remnants on my shirt.

[It was there, and there, and there and there— and I was laughing through my teeth.]]]]

[This certain room was made of me. Parts, at least, of my expulsions, my teeming refuse—all my ruin. The floor was packed and polished, crushed of all the stuff I'd sneezed, the years of sick, the tissued gumming. The walls were made of teeth. Teeth I'd lost, helped by my father's long forefingers toddling each canine and molar back and forth. Teeth I'd had slit into my skin once by dogs hid in the night. Teeth I'd swallowed in my sleep. Down from the ceiling (made of marrow) hung light fixtures strung with splayed-end braids of my cut hair— *along the hair the notes vibrated*—bulbs sat in little crowns made with my nail growths, curved weird and yellow, gummy stunk. The air hung wet with spit and rupture. The desks and dressers stuck together with my eyelashes, with my urine, dandruff, my booboos, sheets of blood, with crusty sleep brushed from my eyelids in the morning of no sun.

[Around the room in glossy bone-made frames hung a long array of photos made of me at many ages, versions I'd already lost again to other rooms. There were the glossy segments of my ultrasound, from nubby up to fist-sized. There were close-clipped renditions of me in grade school, one for each year, a little longer in the neck as time went longer, the minor rash creeping up and out from my school dress. That same dress I wore for years and years, loosening the hemline as I stretched, the moth-holes patched with bits of bedclothes, old newspaper, puppy hair, or whatever other crap that I could muster when my mother would not sew.

[*Hello.*

[Where the timeline of my short schooling ended, the photographs went on. There, me, while shouting, squatting, climbing trees, using a wrench to pull the sink apart and clear the bugs out from the pipes, wading through the muck in our front yard ever-higher, cleaning the mirror with my tongue. The most recent photos had been taken, as far as I could tell, on this cold day. Of me curled inside the room of windows, looking outward, my eyes as gone as anyone.]

[Through the floor the room made of my excess began to vibrate in the sound.]]]

[In the house my breath became a curtain. In the curtain there was fear. I could feel it pulse around me with each outtake, and the quickening, the thick. It made my hair curl in the wet of me, soaking in my dew. The room of windows was small and hot now, growing smaller. I felt my innards at my back. Pressed from both sides, I slurred further, through the part of me still me.

[From my lap my voice sponged endless. The voice was tattered full of leak. I didn't sound like who I'd been once. The gears of the cassette deck caught in their looping. The language crimped, becoming drone. *From in the light I touched the light.* I felt a stretch, a stinging tired. I felt some plastic in my mouth. My present voice hung in my throat all wadded and wayward pulsing, wanting out. *I knew the light grew mold inside me.* I didn't want to hear me. I swallowed inward. Swallowed harder. Swallowed all of me that I could reach.]]]

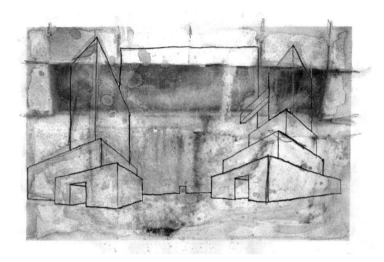

[I was grown. Grown as a woman, yes, but also, grown into the backbone of this house. My head was huge. My lips. My stomach. Every way, I felt my size. Felt my ears burning as I fumbled, slid in my sweat and breath that woke the walls. *And this was mine.*]

[Against the glass I pressed and pummeled, looking for some small way out or in. I scratched my fingers on the surface, felt it scratch back. The glass began to slather. I beat it with my knuckles, elbows, forehead. It would not give. It made no sound. The room for certain had shrunk smaller—making room for other rooms around. The room was going—it was—going—it had me good. I felt the glass against my back—glass through which by now I'd seen the skin of horses, a blub of butter, a woman waddling, gash of tree—it became suddenly more vertical. Its pane edge shrieked against another. The verve vibrated through my neck and belly. The panel I'd had my knees on—through which, another window: wardrobes, peanut butter— stuttered forward, pressing my legs straight, hard enough to make my sockets junk a little, squeam. I heard the sound of stretching muscle. Still I heard the house. My tape-recorder yarbled on—TIKKA LO WENT SHOBBITZ DEET— EYEROID BELDRUM NEENOD PEEPINT CARDKEN SEESUM OIF LIT SHRUM. My voice—my voice—my which one? A pane folded forward for my forehead. It pressed my skull one side here, one side the glass. My brain scrunched in the glimmer. *House*. I found a thought lost of my father—the days that summer, too hot to toddle in the backyard chasing up handfuls of dead bugs, he would lead me through the forest to his shed, where we'd take turns smashing eggs and rattles and glass eyes in his vices—this thought I'd found, though, was of his knee—the way the wrinkles there would make a face. He'd have me speak into it and it spoke back—that ruined knee's cramming voice—*oh fucker*—the voice like mine now in the tape deck screwed and slow—my mutter slurred into molasses—the deck itself caught on the glass—the plastic splintered in the scrunching—the short shards scratching my small hand—one puzzle lodged in my thumb knuckle, squeaking—and again I began to bleed. Bled like those mornings with my head soaked on the pillow all teenaged, my nostrils slickened, my vision white. Bled like those days when I was twenty and my whole womb's load would splot out of me at once, and then again in repetition—in repetition—in—in—and. And. Bled like when even younger I cut my finger there in father's shed and he'd take it in his mouth and suck and suck. Bleeding on the glass now, slid in slow strokes streaking, all bubbling in pools. A slow baptism, puddled in my teeth and belly button. Pooled in the room the size of me—the room from which now through the windows, through the minute, I could not see anything at all.

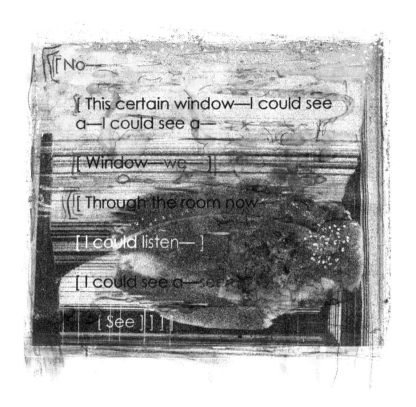

[[No——

[This certain window—I could see
a—I could see a—

[[Window——we   ]]

[[Through the room now——

[I could listen—]

[I could see a——se

[See]]]]

103